Movie Theater
Storybook™

"Blue's Wish" written by Jessica Lissy
"Heart of the Jungle" written by Janice Burgess
Adapted by Ruth Koeppel

CONTENTS

 Blue's Clues
Blue's Wish.. 4

The Backyardigans
Heart of the Jungle... 14

Reader's Digest
Children's Books™

Pleasantville, New York • Montreal, Quebec • Bath, United Kingdom

Blue's Wish

Joe was playing with a model train in the living room.

"All aboard!" called Joe. "We're playing trains. *Chug-a-chug-a-chug-a-chug-a choo choo…*"

Joe chugged over to Blue, who was building a whole train world.

"Train's coming, Blue!" said Joe.

DISK 1
1

4

Joe placed the train on the tracks. Blue made engine noises as she pushed the train along. The train rolled off the tracks and behind the toy chest.

Blue pushed the toy chest aside. The train stood by a little door in the wall. The door shimmered.

"I didn't know there was a door here!" said Joe. "What do you think is inside? Let's see!"

Joe watched as Blue opened the door. Out came a glowing purple wand, surrounded by glittering sparkles.

"Hi! I'm Wish!" said the wand. "Today is your Wish Day. All day long, I'll make your wishes come true!"

"A whole day of wishes!" Joe exclaimed. "What should we wish for first?" Joe looked around the room and the train caught his eye. "Let's wish to be small! Then we can take a train ride. That's a good wish, right? Yeah!"

"Okay," said Wish. She did a little dance while she sang, "Wish, wish, wish come true!"

There was a burst of sparkles. Suddenly, Joe and Blue were tiny enough to get on the train.

"Look how small we are!" said Joe.

The train moved toward them.

"All aboard!" called out Joe.

6

Blue and Joe jumped on. The train got to the top of the hill.

"Here we go—wa-hooo!" shouted Joe as the car hurtled downward.

"Blue, do you want to make a wish?" Joe asked.

Blue barked her agreement. She thought for a moment. Then she made a pawprint.

"We'll play Blue's Clues to figure it out," said Joe. "Great! I love playing Blue's Clues!"

7

Joe and Blue walked over to Sidetable Drawer. They only came up to her legs! Sidetable looked down at them.

"You're tiny!" she said.

"Isn't it great?" said Joe. "Can we have our Handy Dandy Notebook, please?"

"Okay," said Sidetable. When the Notebook dropped, Joe tried to pick it up.

"I'm too small to lift our Handy Dandy Notebook," he said. "We'd better go back to our regular size. How do we do that?"

Wish appeared. "To make the wish end, just touch your pinky to your nose," she told Joe.

Joe held up his pinky.

"Pinky—nose!"

Ding! Joe went back to his regular size. "It worked!" said Joe. He picked up the Handy Dandy Notebook.

"I wonder where we'll find our first clue," he said to himself. He looked around outside.

A giant pawprint covered the entire backyard. "How did I miss that?" Joe wondered. Then he began to draw the backyard in the Handy Dandy Notebook. "What could Blue wish for with our backyard? We'd better find more clues," he said when he was done.

DISK 2
9

Joe went into the kitchen. "You know, I really wish we could find another clue." In a flash, Wish appeared and left a clue on the counter—a bucket with ice inside. Wish disappeared again.

10

Joe looked around the kitchen. "Is there a clue? Oh, on that ice. How did that get there?"

Joe opened his Notebook. "Let's draw ice. One cube, and another cube. So our first clue was the backyard and now our second clue is ice. What could Blue's wish be, with the backyard and ice?" Joe paused. "Let's find another clue to be sure."

Joe walked around the house, searching for the last clue. Behind him, a pawprint began to swoop back and forth.

"Oh, third clue!" called Joe. "Where are you?" Finally, Joe spotted the pawprint. "There it is! Gliding is our third clue! You know what we need now? Our Handy Dandy Notebook!

"Let's draw an arrow this way and an arrow that way to show gliding. We have all three clues to figure out what Blue's wish is! It's time to sit in our..."

 Joe ran to the Thinking Chair.

"Our clues are the backyard, ice, and gliding. What if we were in the backyard, and there was lots and lots of ice? And what if Blue were gliding back and forth, on top of the ice?"

As he thought, Joe pretended to glide in his chair.

"Ice skating!" Joe cried. "Blue's wish is to go ice skating in our backyard! We just figured out Blue's Clues! We're really smart."

11

Blue appeared, barking with excitement.

"Let's go make your wish come true!" said Joe, following Blue out to the backyard. "Ready? Oh, Wi-iish!"

Wish appeared. "I'm here! So...what's Blue's wish?"

"Blue wants to go ice skating—right here in the backyard!" Joe told Wish.

"What a great wish!" said Wish. "Let's all sing together, Wish, wish, wish come true, come true!"

Ding! Instantly the backyard turned into a skating rink. Joe and Blue found there were ice skates on their feet!

15

"We're ice skating!" shouted Joe. "Oh, it's cold. I wish we had warm hats. And hot cocoa! I wish it would snow!"

Ding! It started to snow. The flakes clung to the wool of their warm hats. Blue and Joe skated around, drank hot cocoa and enjoyed the snow.

16

"It was nice visiting you!" called Wish. "Hope you liked your wishes!"

"Thanks, Wish," Joe said with a wave. "Thanks for making our wishes come true!"

The BACKYARDIGANS

Heart of the Jungle

DISK 1
1

"I'm Tarzan. I live in the jungle and I can talk to animals. That's why they call me Tarzan of the Animals." Tyrone beat his chest and yelled, "Ooohh-oh-oooh-oh!"

Tyrone and his friends loved to play in the backyard area their houses shared.

His best friend Pablo came over. "You're Tarzan, aren't you?"

"I certainly am Tarzan," agreed Tyrone.

"I'm Tarzan, too," said Pablo.

"Really?" asked Tyrone.

Pablo nodded. "Tarzan the Strong. I live in the jungle, I swing on vines, and of course, I do this..." He beat his chest and yodeled, "Ooohh-oh-oooh-oh!"

As Tyrone and Pablo beat their chests, their friend Austin hopped into the yard.

"You Tarzan?" he asked them.

"I'm Tarzan of the Animals," said Tyrone.

 "I'm Tarzan the Strong," put in Pablo.

"Me Tarzan, too," said Austin.

"Are you Tarzan who doesn't say too much?" asked Pablo.

Austin nodded. "Ooooh-oh-oooh-oh-ooooh!" he sang out, beating his chest.

"Hey, there!" called out a voice. It was Uniqua.

"You Tarzan, too?" Austin asked her.

"I'm Professor Uniqua, the brilliant scientist," she said. "Look what I just discovered!" She held up a tiny creature. The Tarzans gathered around.

"I've never seen anything like it," said Tyrone.

"He's a Worman," Uniqua told them. "His name is Sherman."

"Him look...sad," said Austin.

"He can't find the other Wormans," said Uniqua.

"Where do you think he comes from?" asked Pablo.

"That's the next thing I'm going to discover, so I can take him home," she said.

"I could ask him where he lives," said Tyrone. "I can talk to animals, you know."

Tyrone made squeaky worman noises. Sherman made squeaky worman noises back.

"He says he's from deep in the heart of the jungle," said Tyrone, "where there are lots of tall trees."

"And vines," added Austin.

"And beautiful flowers," finished Uniqua.

As they spoke, the yard around them began to change into a tropical paradise.

6 ▷ Uniqua, dressed in an explorer outfit, made her way through the thick tropical growth carrying Sherman.

7 ▷ Tyrone, Pablo, and Austin swung by on vines.

"Which way to the heart of the jungle, Sherman?" asked Uniqua. "Let's go this way," she called to the Tarzans. She set off down the jungle trail. "Here's an excellent place to look for the Wormans."

"We should get out of here," said Tyrone. "There may be can't-see-ums."

"Can't-see-ums bad bugs," said Austin.

"I don't see anything," said Uniqua.

"That's why they're called can't-see-ums," Pablo told her.

Buzzing filled the air. Uniqua slapped at her neck.

"Let's go before the can't-see-ums find us!" said Pablo. The buzzing grew louder.

"Run!" cried Tyrone.

The Tarzans took off, pursued by a ball of buzzing bugs. Uniqua jumped in with a bottle of bug spray. "Stop tickling those Tarzans!" she cried.

"You got rid of the can't-see-ums," approved Tyrone.

"Come on. We still haven't found the heart of the jungle," said Uniqua.

"Are we close to your home yet, Sherman?" asked Tyrone.

Sherman looked around. A big

11 raindrop landed on him. Soon it was pouring. Uniqua pulled out an umbrella. The Tarzans huddled underneath.

12 The clearing began to fill with water. The friends piled onto a giant leaf and sailed downstream. Suddenly, the sound of rushing water filled the air.

"It's a giant waterfall!" yelled Pablo.

13 Uniqua hooked her umbrella onto an overhanging vine. "We'll swing over to the bank!" she cried.

"You need a strong Tarzan for this, and I'm Tarzan the Strong," said Pablo. He heaved them onto the bank.

14 Now the sun filtered through the tall trees. Sherman picked his head up and chirped.

"We're close!" Tyrone said.

"Listen," said Uniqua.

15 Sherman chirped again. Worman voices chirped in reply. Sherman was home! "Bye, Sherman!" The Tarzans and Uniqua waved good-bye. "We'll miss you!"

Uniqua thanked the Tarzans for all their help.

The Tarzans yelled and beat **16** their chests. After a moment, Uniqua joined them. Just then, Austin's stomach growled.

"You know what that means," said Pablo. "Snacktime!" They all started for home.

"That was a very Tarzany adventure, don't you think?" asked Tyrone.

"Ooohh-oh-oooh-oh," the Tarzans sang out one last time.